Text and illustrations
copyright © 2013
by Onur Tukel

All rights reserved
Amazon Publishing
Attn: Amazon Children's Publishing
P.O. Box 400818
Las Vegas, NV 89140
www.amazon.com/amazonchildrenspublishing

Library of Congress Cataloging-in-Publication Data available upon request.

9781477816554 (hardcover)
9781477866559 (e-book)

The illustrations were hand-drawn in pencil, outlined with ink,
scanned and colored digitally.
Book design by Katrina Damkoehler
Editor: Margery Cuyler

Printed in China (R)
First edition
10 9 8 7 6 5 4 3 2 1

RAINSTACK!

By **ONUR TUKEL**

AMAZON CHILDREN'S PUBLISHING

Dedicated to my big brothers,
Uf & Timur

It hadn't rained in months.
The valley was dusty and dry.
The animals were hot and thirsty.
If it didn't rain soon, the animals might not survive.

"All the grass is gone," said the zebra. "How will we graze?"

"The river has turned to puddles," said the monkey. "Soon we'll have nothing to drink."

"If it doesn't rain soon, we're doomed," cried the beaver. "What will we do?"

"Everyone please calm down," said the lion.
"If we work together, I'm sure we will come up
    with a solution."

"What if we try shaking the rain out of the sky?" said the fox.

"How would we do that?" asked the hippo.

"We could try jumping up and down," said the elephant.

So the animals jumped.

But no rain fell.

"We mustn't quit," said the lion. "If we keep
  thinking, we'll come up with another solution."
"It's no use," said the monkey.
"Don't give up hope," said the zebra.
"That's right," said the giraffe. "Keep your chins up!"
"That's easy for you to say," said the fox.

Meanwhile a rabbit was watching from the top of the hill.

I bet I can come up with a solution on my own, he thought.

Now *this* rabbit was nothing like the other animals in the valley. *This* rabbit was an inventor.

Not so long ago, the animals had
picked fruit as a group . . .

. . . until *this* rabbit made a device
that picked the fruit for them.

When it was cold, the elephants
had blown warm air into the valley
with their trunks . . .

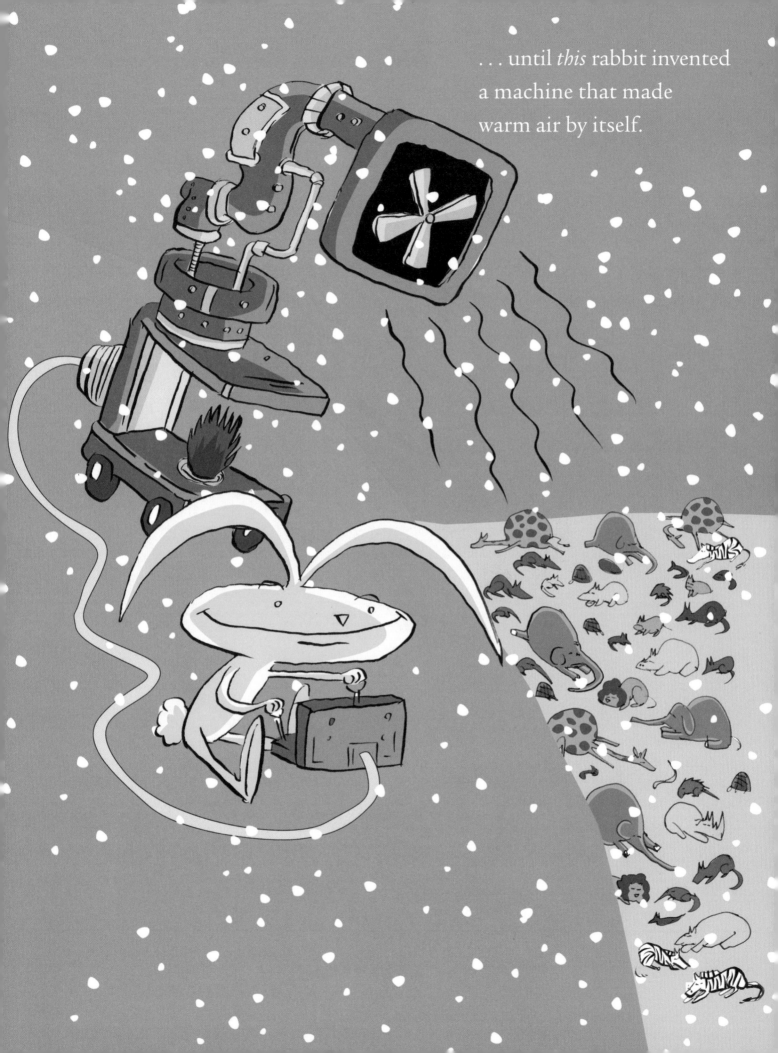

. . . until *this* rabbit invented
a machine that made
warm air by itself.

When it rained, the animals had gathered water
from the river and pushed it to the valley . . .

until *this* rabbit made a pipe . . .

. . . that brought the water to them.

But now the river was dry.
Soon there would be no water left.

"What a disaster!" cried the monkey. "First we're going to starve, then we're going to wilt away into nothing!"

"No, we're not," said the rabbit.

"Yes, we are!"

"Listen to me for a moment," said the rabbit. "I'm going to invent a robot that will make it rain!"

The animals grew silent.
They waited for the rabbit to explain.

"Every problem can be fixed with science,"
said the rabbit. "And when I'm finished,
my robot will work!"

"My mother used to say that every
problem can be fixed with teamwork,"
said the elephant. "Maybe we can help."

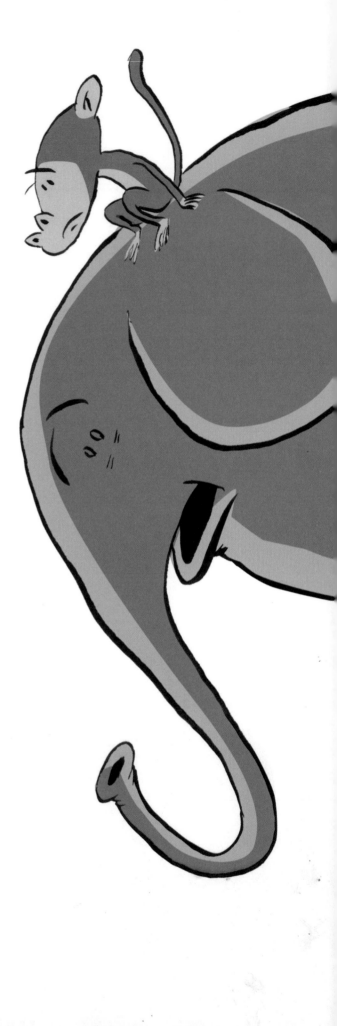

"Thanks, but I don't need any help," said the rabbit.
"I can do this on my own."
"How exciting," yelled the giraffe. "The rabbit's
 rain-making robot is going to fix everything!"
"Let's party!" said the monkey.

Finally the robot was finished. The animals
crowded around to have a look.
"How does it work?" asked the rhino.

"It's simple," said the rabbit. "Imagine a cloud over our heads. That cloud is made up of tiny raindrops.

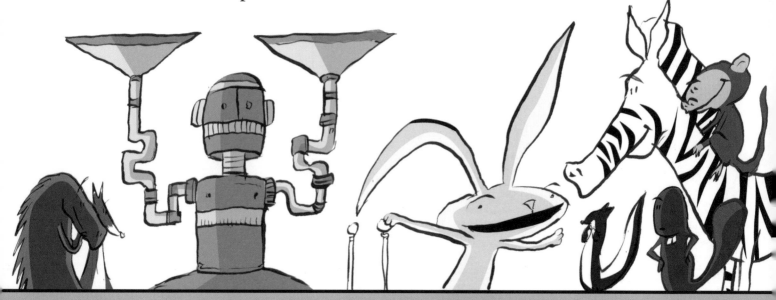

Now imagine the robot pumping warm air into the cloud. This will cause the raindrops to grow heavy."

"Does the robot run on batteries?" asked the wolf.
"Or gasoline?" asked the fox.
"No, those things aren't good for the planet,"
said the rabbit. "My robot runs on carrot juice!"

This worried the animals.

They had eaten almost all of their food.

Nothing remained but a small pile of carrots.

The rabbit spent the next few days testing the robot.
This took lots of carrots.

The animals watched the pile grow smaller . . .

and smaller . . .

and smaller.

At last, the robot was ready.

"Tomorrow, I'll drive the robot to the top of the mountain," said the rabbit.

"Why?" asked the giraffe.

"To get it close to the clouds," said the rabbit.

"When I turn on the robot, it will make rain."

"Can we come with you?" asked the turtle. "You might need our help."

"You might all slow me down," said the rabbit. "*Especially* you!"

"We can keep up," said the turtle.

"I doubt it," said the rabbit. "But if you want to come along, I won't stop you."

The next day, all the animals in the valley
followed the rabbit up the mountain.

When they reached the top, the rabbit wasted no time.
He turned on the robot and pulled its levers.
"*Sssssshhhhhh,*" the robot hissed as warm air shot from its vents.

The warm air rose very slowly.
"It's never going to reach those clouds,"
said the monkey.
"Please be patient," said the rabbit.

The animals waited and waited as the warm air rose up and up and up. Just as it reached the clouds, the robot made a strange noise.

SPITTLE, **POP**, **BANG**.

The robot sputtered and shook until . . .

BUMPITY,
BUMP,
BUMP,
BUMP.

It rolled all the way down the mountain.
"Oh no!" cried the animals.

"We've run out of fuel," said the rabbit.
"This is stressing me out," cried the monkey.

"There's only one carrot left," said the rabbit. "It's not enough to drive the robot back up the mountain!"

"It's hopeless," said the monkey.

"Maybe you're right," agreed the rabbit.

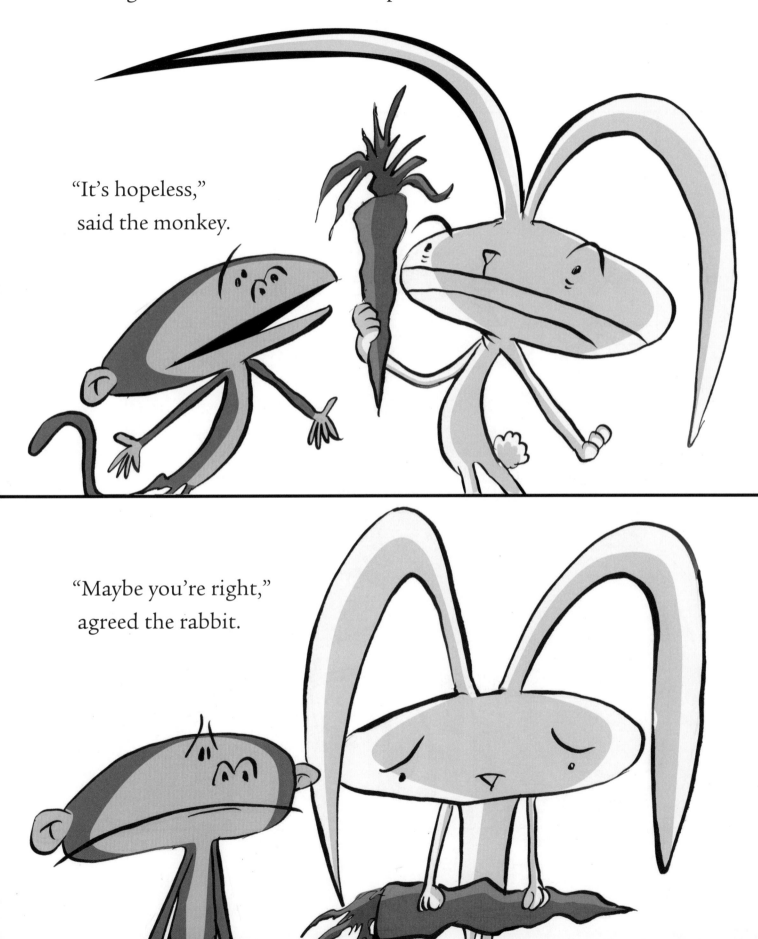

"Wait a minute," said the lion. "Remember how we used to bring water to the valley? If we all work together, we can push the robot back up the mountain."

And that's just what they did.
It wasn't easy. The robot was much
heavier than it looked. But they pushed
and pushed and *puuuuushed* until they
reached the top.

The rabbit shouted, "We must get the robot as close to the clouds as possible!"

The zebra remembered how
the animals used to pick fruit.
"Let's lift the robot into the sky,"
he said.

"It weighs a ton and the clouds are too high,"
said the monkey. "It'll never happen."
"It will if we all work together," said the zebra.

So the animals lifted the robot.

Then they lifted each other.

Up they went!

UP! UP! **UP!**

Soon they were almost touching the clouds!
"We made it!" shouted the rabbit.

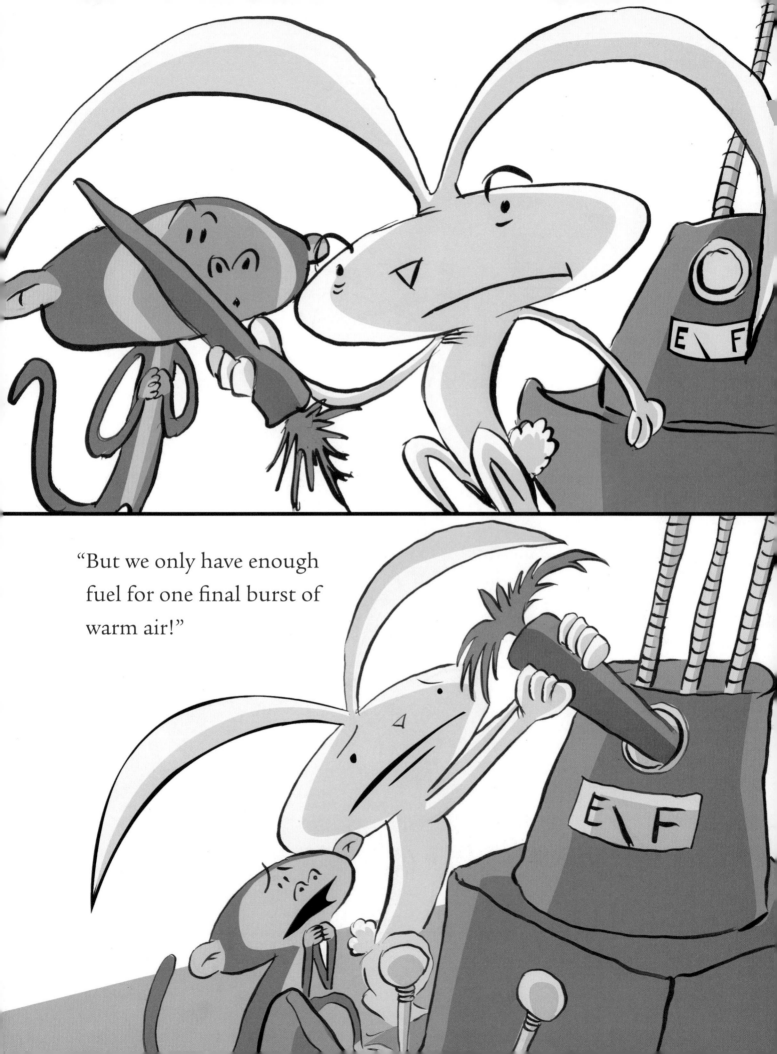

"But we only have enough fuel for one final burst of warm air!"

Warm air streamed out of the robot.
The clouds rumbled.

The animals cheered!

"We need more warm air!"
called the rabbit.

The elephants remembered how they once
warmed the valley in the winter.
"We can help!" they trumpeted.

The elephants pulled themselves up
from the bottom of the pile.

When they reached the top, the rabbit shouted,
"Great job! Now blow!"

The elephants each took a deep breath . . .

. . . and blew!

The stack swayed
from the weight
of the elephants.

First it rocked left!

Then it rocked right!

And then . . .

The animals were too shocked to move.
The robot lay in pieces all around them.
Their plan had almost worked. Now they were
out of options.

"It's all over," the monkey said.

And then . . .

It started to rain!